# The Six Horse

### Written By
### Shani T. Night

*Infinite Generations Publishing*

ISBN: 978-1-953364-03-6

Photography By Canva

 Produced and Published by Infinite Generations
137 National Harbor, Suite 300, MD 20745

www.infinitegenerations.com

Special Thanks to my inspiration and Love of my life—my husband.

A special thanks to my daughter, who's courage and inspiration is my leading light.

To my sons, you inspire me to live out loud.

To my parents, without you, my life would not have been possible. You are the best.

## Dear Reader:

Thank you for your purchase.
I hope you enjoy The Six Horse.

Please share a review of this book on Amazon.

Visit my website for discounts, contests, and/or giveaways.
www.shanitnight.com

*Follow Shani Night:*
 instagram.com/shaninight
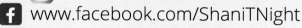 www.facebook.com/ShaniTNight

# *Preparation*

Hi, my name is Shani!

Today is the big day.  The biggest day
of the year for my family. I live on a
family farm and I have a pet horse.
My mom has a favorite horse too.
Her name is Dasey.

Well, the six horse is not my pet but he's my favorite horse.  I try to take care of him every day but I'm only six, so I can only do so much.

I love my six horse. I know when he eats, sleeps, and plays.  My dad is training him, so most days he's up before dawn.

If you're wondering why today is so big, it's family race day! Today is our family's annual horse race. This is when we race our favorite horses.

The six horse is my favorite horse, and I know he's going to win.

I instinctively know it.

I know because he winked at me, which said, "I'll win for you today."

I love everything about horses, but I especially love the good luck my six horse brings. My brother has a lucky horse, he says.

His favorite horse is the five horse, and he's always picking his horse over mine. Today is no different. He doesn't want my horse to win but he doesn't know my secret.

The six horse gave me a special wink, so I know he'll win today.

I believe my six horse knows me and can recognize my voice.  He hears me coming in the morning and he looks my way.  He never looks at my brother (I don't think), so I know he recognizes my voice.

He also knows when I'm sad or when I'm mad, my six horse is special for sure.

He communicates with me in a lot of ways.  Sometimes I can hear him nick-ering.  He doesn't squeal a lot when I'm around, so I'll need to figure that out.

He makes other sounds that do not sound happy.  He can snort, grunt, and groan but I've never heard him cry.
Do horses cry?  I don't think so.

He doesn't make a lot of noise but when he does, I know it's for a reason.

When he's out and about, I can hear a neigh, and sometimes the other horses respond. He uses his ears, neck, and head movement to talk to me. There's a lot foot stomping and tail swishing, but I can talk about that another day. Today, my six horse is A-okay.

My dad says, I'm good with the six horse because I've taken the time to teach him and he's taught me. We know each other very well and that's what makes us friends.

I've gained his trust and he's gained mine and that's what really matters.

I've learned that when his ears are relaxed, he's bored or resting.

When his lower lip is loose, he's relaxed. I've also learned that when he gives me a wink, we're going to have a good day. Like today!

There are other secrets I've learned, but I'll have to save that too for another day. Today is race day.

Today, I need to make sure my six horse stays on his routine, and I give him his favorite treats. Like clockwork, my dad is up and out early to take care of my horse.

His morning workouts are important. They're going to tell me a lot about how my horse is doing today.

# *His Gear*

He needs a lot of equipment. The basic saddle and bridle, just won't do.

He needs a lot of special items, like ear plugs, blinkers, tongue ties, and shadow rolls to name a few. Most importantly, he needs shoes and they are called horse-shoes.

Don't forget his feeding and grooming supplies but we can talk about that on another adventure.

Now that I've covered the basics, it's time for the family race.

I'm not really sure why we have this race every year, but this year my horse was allowed to join, so I'm excited.

# The Race

## They're off!

The start of the race is always the most stressful. My brother feels that if your horse does not have a good start, he will have no chance to win. I do not agree.

I think you can recover from anything, even a bad start. I think! Where there's a will, there's a way. That's what my parents tell me.

*Now for what is important during the race.*

The location of where my horse is on the track is really important. This particular race doesn't last that long and every mile marker counts.

# Here's the mile-fraction marker:

*7/8 mile* - He's in last place but I know this is his trick.

I'm not worried at all.  Why, you ask?

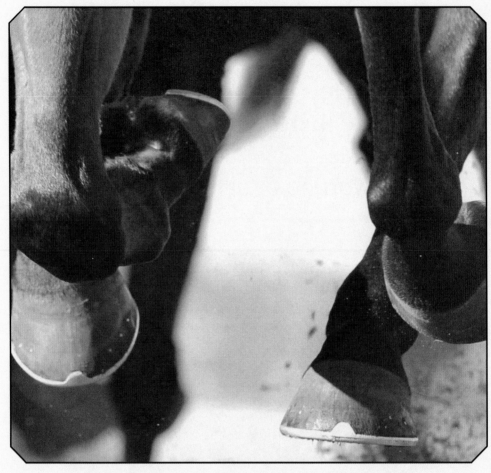

**_He's fast and furious and able._**

My six horse is a closer. He starts slow but he ends fast. Plus, this race is at the right time of day for him.

We've trained for this and we're ready to go. We have luck on our side because horses are just lucky. This particular race, my horse can run in his sleep.

Not to mention, the track is dirt and he does well here. Plus dirt races are typically faster, at least that's what my dad says. I'm glad it's not muddy today. Whew!

*5/8 mile* - He's making his move.

He's getting his legs and quite nicely. The six horse is settling in and gaining the lead.

He's realizing that he can do it. He can win, if he tries. Then again, he does this all the time. This is how he races.

*3/8 mile* - He gained the lead, which I knew he would.

He has found his speed, which is his strength.

Oh wow!

Look at him go.  Look at him shine.

# The Winner

*And the winner is the six horse!*

I'm not shocked he won. We've worked hard and prepared for this day for so long.

We put in the time and preparation for this dream to come true.

Thank you six horse!

You are special in every way, and that is A-okay with me.

I wonder what's next. Will there be more races?

# *The Victory Lap*

I'm so happy for the six horse!

He found his confidence today, and he knows he can win.

Last year, I watched the victory lap and I dreamed of the six horse winning. My dream was not for the win alone, but for the experience of it all.

### *The excitement!*

### *The thrill!*

### *And knowing that we can do anything!*

That is how I feel today.  I feel as if I can conquer the world because I tried, because we tried.

We've worked hard all year for this moment, and I couldn't have shared it with a better friend. *The six horse!*

# Inspiration

I'm so happy for the six horse. He found his confidence today, and he knows he can win.

I think this is what life is about.

Discovering yourself, trying to be the best you can be, and being surrounded by loved ones. Being inspired by those we love and who love us.

Enjoying special moments with family and friends. Do you have any ideas about life?

What Inspires you?

What a long day. My six horse won today. All of my care for him has paid off, and I'm so proud of him today, as always.

Thank you six horse for giving me a victory today.

I'll let you rest in your favorite spot, but I'll see you tomorrow.

Tomorrow will come and we'll start anew.
What will be our next adventure?

*P.S. I didn't forget about those secrets.*
*I'll have to write about that next time, and*
*include the celebration. Today has been a*
*long day!*

# The
# End

**Other Books In The Six Horse Series**